TEN LITTLE PRINCESSES

MIKE BROWNLOW · SIMON RICKERTY

ORCHARD

Ten little princesses, going to the ball,

Trotting on their ponies, past the castle wall.

Are they looking forward to their very special day?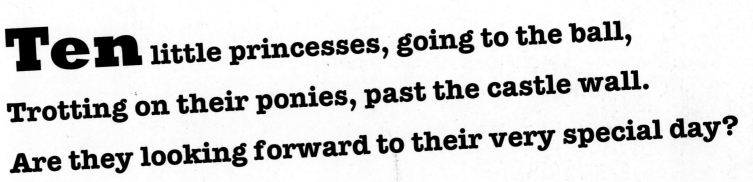

Ten little princesses all shout,

"Yay!"

Ten little princesses, looking quite divine.

"Ouch!"

– a princess pricks her thumb.

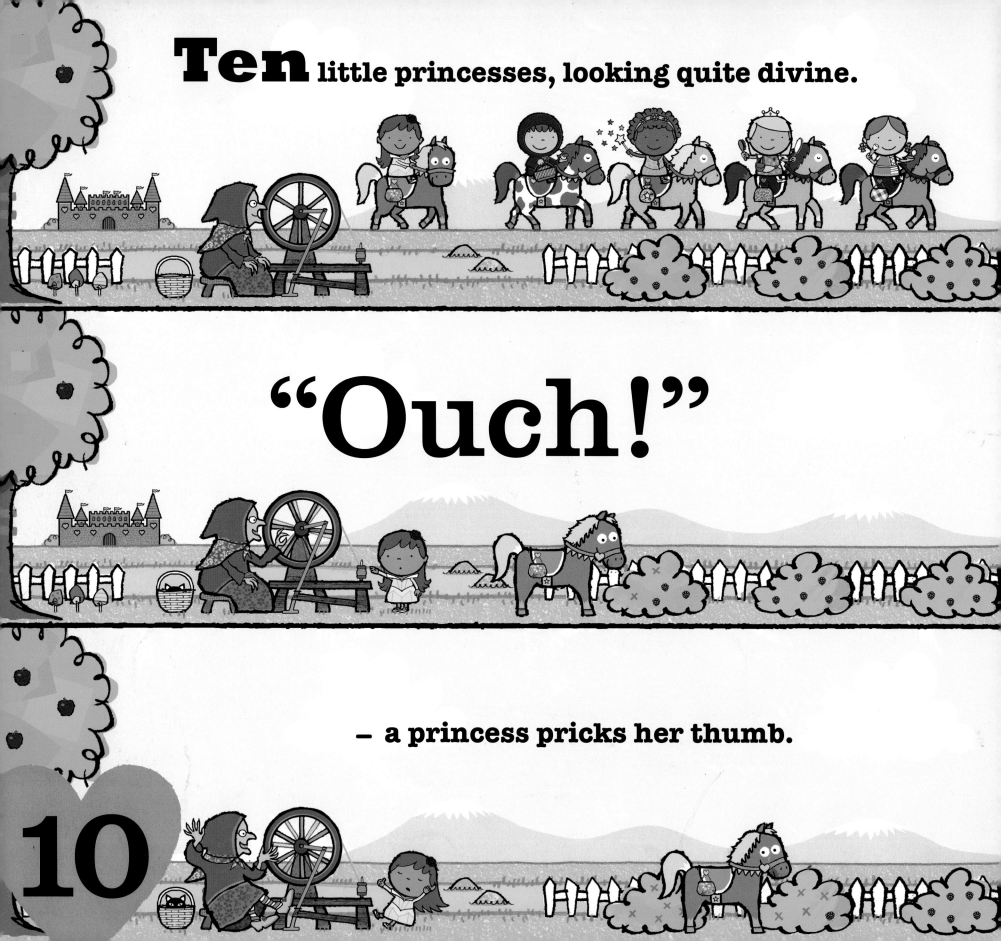

Now there are . . .

"Crunch!"

goes the poisoned apple.

Now there are . . .

. . . eight.

Eight little princesses pass a prince who's heaven.

"Hi,"

smiles the charming prince.

8

Now there are . . .

seven

7

Seven little princesses hide behind some sticks.

"Huff!" blows a big bad wolf.

Now there are . . .

. . . **six.**

Six little princesses, trying to survive.

"Kissy, kissy?" begs a frog.

6

Now there are . . .

. . . **five.**

5

Five little princesses spot a hairy paw.

"You're a beauty," growls the Beast.

Now there are . . .

. . . **four.**

**Four little princesses
climb a beanstalk tree.**

4

"Fee-fie-foe!"

a giant says.

Now there are . . .

. . . three.

3

Three little princesses, really in a stew.

Whoosh!

roars a dragon's breath.

Now there are . . .

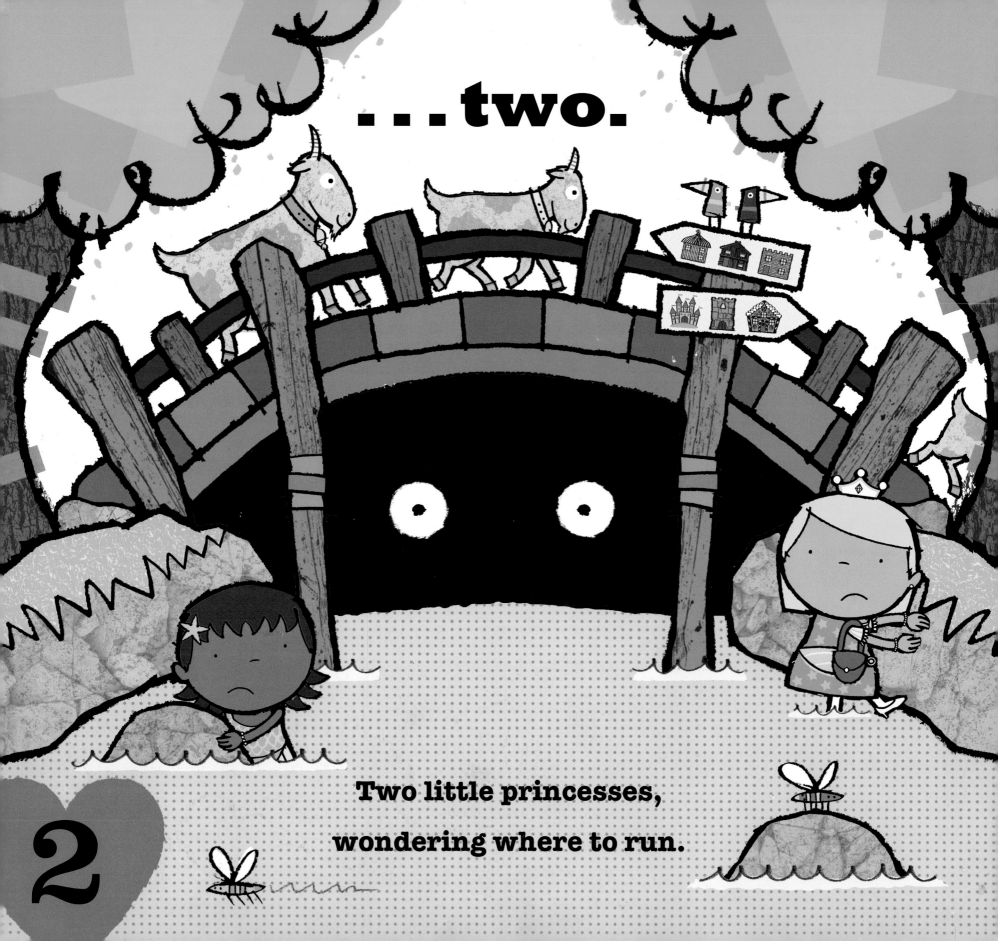

. . . two.

2

Two little princesses,
wondering where to run.

"Grrrr!"

snarls a sneaky troll.
Now there is . . .

One little princess, feeling sad and blue.

All her friends have disappeared.

Whatever can she do?

One little princess
makes a special call . . .
She rings her Fairy God Mum
on her mobile crystal ball.

Fairy God Mum waves her wand . . .

the others reappear!

The baddies run, the ball is saved.

It's time to whoop and cheer!

Are they feeling happy
as they dance the night away?

For my own little princesses,
Dilly, Rachel, Sally and Catie
M.B.

For Erin and Isla
S.R.

ORCHARD BOOKS
338 Euston Road
London NW1 3BH
Orchard Books Australia
Level 17/207 Kent Street, Sydney, NSW 2000

First published in 2014 by Orchard Books

ISBN 978 1 40833 010 4

3 5 7 9 10 8 6 4 2

Printed in China

Orchard Books is a division of Hachette Children's Books,
an Hachette UK company
www.hachette.co.uk